MARYA KHAN

⚑ AND THE ⚑

AWESOME ADVENTURE PARK

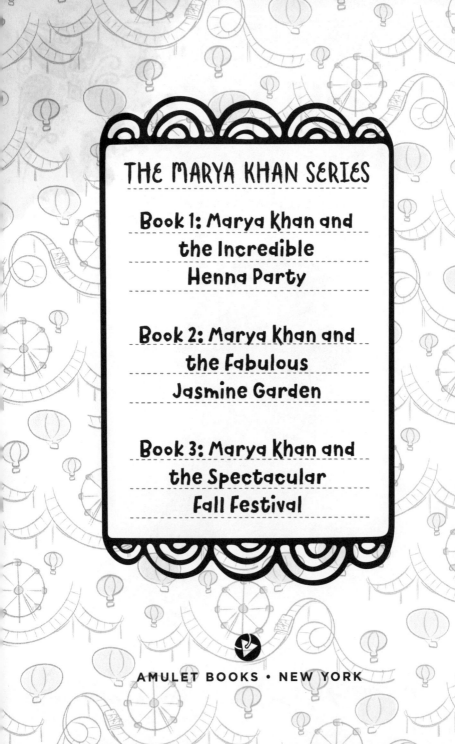

AMULET BOOKS · NEW YORK

MARYA KHAN

AND THE
AWESOME ADVENTURE PARK

written by
SAADIA FARUQI

illustrated by
ANI BUSHRY

Cataloging-in-Publication Data has been applied for and may be obtained from the Library of Congress.

ISBN 978-1-4197-6122-5

Text © 2024 Saadia Faruqi
Illustrations © 2024 Ani Bushry Illustration LLC
Book design by Deena Micah Fleming

Printed and bound in U.S.A.
10 9 8 7 6 5 4 3 2 1

Amulet Books are available at special discounts when purchased in quantity for premiums and promotions as well as fundraising or educational use. Special editions can also be created to specification. For details, contact specialsales@abramsbooks.com or the address below.

ABRAMS The Art of Books
195 Broadway, New York, NY 10007
abramsbooks.com

FOR MY
KIDS,
WHO LOVE
ADVENTURE
PARKS

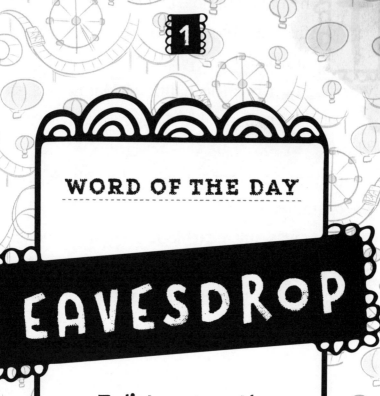

1

WORD OF THE DAY

EAVESDROP

To listen secretly

The most horrible thing happened on the first day of spring break. I went downstairs to get a glass of water, and guess what I saw from the hallway? Mama was sitting at the kitchen table drinking tea with Mrs. Rhodes.

In case you didn't know, Mrs. Rhodes was Alexa's mom.

Alexa was my next-door neighbor, and she was also in my third-grade class. She was super rich and super annoying and had a super-strange fashion sense because she wore fancy dresses and bows in her hair all day long.

She was my sort-of friend, so those things didn't bother me.

Mostly.

Only now her mom was in my house. For the first time ever.

With my mama. It was strange.

What were they even laughing about? I crept closer to the kitchen door to eavesdrop.

I have a very cool journal that teaches me a

new big word every day. A few days ago, my Word of the Day was *eavesdrop*. That means to overhear a secret conversation.

And guess what? You hear a lot of very interesting things when you eavesdrop.

For example, yesterday I found out that Baba had a dentist appointment coming up soon, and he was really scared about it. He thought he had a cavity or something.

A cavity meant your tooth got sick and disgusting because you didn't brush your teeth enough.

Ew. I loved my baba, but I didn't want to see any disgusting teeth, no thank you very much.

Also, another example. My older brother, Salman—we call him Sal—was failing social studies, and he hadn't told anyone yet except his best friend. I grinned to myself. I couldn't wait until the next parent-teacher conference. Sal was going to be in so much trouble!

And now, here I was, eavesdropping again. I leaned forward and peeked into the room, just like a detective.

"Spring break has started," Mrs. Rhodes said as she sipped some tea. I knew those mugs. They were big and white, and they said KEEP CALM AND DRINK CHAI. They were Mama's favorite mugs, and she only took them out on special occasions.

I guess Mrs. Rhodes visiting us on a Monday morning was pretty special.

"Does Alexa have any plans?" Mama asked.

"That's what I wanted to talk to you about," Mrs. Rhodes said in a mysterious voice.

My detective-ears twitched. What was she going to say?

Only grown-ups have a very weird way of talking. Instead of saying something interesting, Mrs. Rhodes started talking about her job. She was on the city council, but I'm not sure what she actually did there. I imagined her sitting in meetings with a notepad in her lap. She always looked very important.

And busy. One time she missed her own

daughter's birthday party because of her job.

That's the only time I ever felt bad for Alexa.

I got bored and felt a yawn coming in my mouth. Oh no! My eyes scrunched up and my chest swelled and my jaw flew wide open like a lion getting ready to swallow a whole deer.

I tried my best to stop, but it was too late.

YAWN!

Ooh, that felt good. But then I realized I'd yawned too loud. Mama and Mrs. Rhodes had stopped talking.

"Marya, is that you?" Mama called out.

I walked slowly into the kitchen, looking down at my feet. Even I knew eavesdropping was frowned upon. "Hello, Mrs. Rhodes," I mumbled.

"Oh hello, dear," she replied. "Alexa was wondering where you were."

That's when I looked up very fast. How had I missed the third person sitting at my kitchen table? It was Alexa, grinning very big. She wore a blue satin dress and ate from a plate of cookies.

Chocolate chip, my favorite.

Alexa wiped her mouth with a napkin and said, "Hi, Marya!"

I stared at her. What was she doing here, that's what I'd like to know.

Mama gave me a nudge, and I stumbled. "He-hello."

Alexa picked up the plate and offered it to me. "Would you like a cookie?" she asked. "They're delicious."

"No thanks," I replied. Did she forget they were *my* cookies? Baba got them from the grocery store yesterday. I knew exactly how delicious they were.

"Why don't you girls go play for a while?" Even though Mama said it like a question, I knew it was really a command. Mama was like that. When she said something in that sharp tone, it meant I needed to obey her.

Too bad I had no idea what we would play. It's not like I had a ton of toys in my room.

Mama was giving me angry eyes, so I grabbed a cookie and nodded to Alexa. "Come on!"

We left the moms in the kitchen and went upstairs.

"This is so much fun, Marya," Alexa said excitedly. "I can't believe we're having a playdate."

I rolled my eyes. "Playdates are for babies."

"Okay, friendship date then?"

I laughed, which meant cookie crumbs went everywhere. "That sounds even worse."

Alexa shrugged. "I think it sounds okay."

We reached my room, and suddenly I got really nervous. Alexa was rich. What was she going to think of my room? She'd been to my house one time before, on my birthday. Except she'd stayed in the backyard on account of my surprise henna party. She'd never seen my room.

I gulped and opened the door. "Well, here it is."

Alexa didn't even look around. She went straight to my bed and flopped onto it like she owned the place. "What should we play, Marya?" she asked.

"Er, I don't know."

She sat up with a grin. "What about Truth or Dare?"

2

WORD OF THE DAY

CHALLENGE

A contest or dare

Truth or Dare? That was a game for big kids. My sister, Aliyah, played it with her friends sometimes, but she was thirteen and scary. She looked like a teenager, but inside she was an evil witch or something. I was almost sure.

I gulped again. "Okay."

Alexa smiled sweetly at me. "Don't worry, we can play the easy version."

I sat down on the edge of the bed. "Easy version?" I said. Or basically, I became a parrot at this point, just repeating whatever she said.

It was a little weird to have Alexa in my room, acting like she belonged here and trying to make me feel less worried. Maybe I was dreaming. Maybe I'd never woken up this morning.

One time I ate way too much pizza. I had a dream that I was in the middle of the sea, on a raft shaped like a pizza. Giant-sized olives floated all around me. Only the olives had big jaws and sharp teeth. It was a horrible dream because olives are super delicious, so they shouldn't be

attacking me. They should be my best friends and live in my tummy.

Alexa snapped her fingers. "Focus, Marya!"

"Sorry," I mumbled. "I was thinking about pizza."

"Ooh, nice. Maybe we can order pizza for lunch."

That made me sit up straight. Pizza was my

favorite food, as long as I didn't eat too much. "I'll go first," I said quickly. "Truth or Dare?"

"Dare, of course."

I looked around the room, trying to find a good dare. Something that would make her shiny blond hair messy and her pretty dress all crumpled up.

Aha! There was a jump rope in the corner. Perfect! "I dare you to jump rope fifteen times without falling."

"Easy!" Alexa rolled her eyes and went to get the jump rope. It was a new one Baba had gotten me for Eid. She picked it up and started jumping and counting. "One. Two. Three . . ."

My mouth dropped open. She was good. She jumped straight in the air, and her dress floated around her like an umbrella. And her hair didn't get even a little bit messy.

"Fifteen!" Alexa finished. "Want me to keep going?"

"Er, no." I took a deep breath. "You were good."

She raised one eyebrow like in the movies. "Surprised?"

"Well, yes," I stammered. "I didn't think you were . . ."

"Athletic?"

I looked at her with very big eyes. "You know what that means?" It means being good at sports, which I knew for two reasons: (a) I was very athletic, and (b) It was in my Word of the Day journal one month ago.

"I'm very athletic," Alexa said proudly. "I have a gym in my basement."

My eyes got even bigger. I couldn't imagine

a gym in someone's house. Only Alexa's house was really a mansion, so maybe it was normal for rich people. "What else can you do?" I asked suspiciously.

"Kickboxing," she replied, flipping her hair. "And crunches."

Crunches made my tummy hurt. "I can run really fast," I told her. "Like, high-speed."

"That's nice," she replied kindly. "I'm not that good at running."

I was pretty sure she was lying, because if someone had a gym in their house, they'd better be good at the basics like running and jumping. Only Alexa was always sugar sweet and nice to everyone, so maybe she was telling the truth.

Alexa leaned against the wall. "I dare you to show me how fast you can run."

My heart thumped. A running dare? In my room? There wasn't enough space, but I didn't want to lose the dare. Whenever Aliyah lost a dare, her face got all red and she screeched like a hungry eagle. I didn't want to be like that.

I took a deep breath. "You got it!"

Alexa clapped her hands. "Okay then!" she squealed happily. "Run all around the room twice, over the bed, then come back right here."

Oh, like an obstacle course! I loved obstacle courses almost as much as pizza.

I zipped to the other end of the room and back, then jumped up on my bed. I took three giant steps—one, two, three—and jumped back down to the floor. From there I twirled around, ran to the center of the room, and jumped over a pile of books Mama kept telling me to put away. Then I stopped suddenly.

Oops, it was my chair, right in the middle of the room. Mama was always telling me to tuck it under my desk. And now I knew the reason why. Chairs in the middle of the room could make me lose a race big-time.

Alexa was looking at her watch. What kind of third grader even wears a watch, that's what I'd like to know. "Eighteen seconds," she said.

My heart beat really fast. That was good, right?

That was less than half a minute. That was nothing, really.

The chair was my last obstacle, and I was gonna crush it like a champion!

I threw myself across the chair and landed on the other side with a whoosh.

Alexa clapped. "Twenty seconds!"

I panted loudly and fell onto the bed. "That was fun!" I said. "Kinda like Skye Adventure Park."

Skye was the best park in the state. It had a cool obstacle course, a giant water park, and roller coasters that went upside down.

Alexa gasped. "You've been to Skye?"

"It's only my most favorite place in the whole world," I told her. "We went last summer when my cousins came from Pakistan."

"It's my favorite too," Alexa breathed. "More than any other place on the planet."

I blinked in shock. Alexa and I actually liked the same place? Who knew?

Also: She liked Skye better than all the other places she'd visited? "Even better than Paris?" I asked. She'd gone there during winter break and then come to class in January and told everyone about it. Three times.

She shrugged like Paris was no big deal. "Oh yeah. Paris was boring. My dad was in meetings all day and my mom only went to the spa. I stayed in the hotel."

I was horrified. "Did you at least see the Eiffel Tower?"

"From my hotel window," Alexa replied. "It's really . . . tall."

I stared at her. That's what she had to say about the Eiffel Tower? It was tall? That was like saying the sun was round. Or that the pyramids in Egypt were triangular.

I knew all about the pyramids because Baba showed them to me once on his computer. They're the most spectacular things in the world. Even more than Skye Adventure Park. If I ever went to Egypt, there's no way I'd sit in the hotel. I'd be out in the desert, staring at the pyramids all day long.

And riding camels. Those were cute.

3

WORD OF THE DAY

CROCHET

Making fabric with

a hooked needle

and yarn

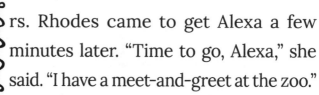rs. Rhodes came to get Alexa a few minutes later. "Time to go, Alexa," she said. "I have a meet-and-greet at the zoo."

I imagined Mrs. Rhodes having a meeting with a bunch of animals. Bears, for sure. Tigers, maybe? Ooh, and penguins. Those were even cuter than camels.

I giggled. Mrs. Rhodes was so not dressed for a zoo meeting.

Mama sent me a look that said, *Marya, behave.* I knew that look very well because everyone in my family used it on me.

"I'll come again tomorrow, okay?" Alexa said cheerfully.

I stopped giggling. "What? Why?"

It wasn't like I hated Alexa or anything. She was okay if you ignored her annoying qualities. But my best friend was Hanna, and that's who I wanted to spend spring break with. Only Hanna's baby sister was sick, and Hanna was helping her mom take care of her.

Bummer.

Mama's *behave* look was even stronger now. "Alexa can hang out here anytime," she assured Mrs. Rhodes.

Alexa smiled so big her cheeks got round. "It'll be fun, Marya Khan! We can do more dares."

I rolled my eyes, but secretly, I was happy. The dares *had* been pretty fun. Maybe we could run obstacles in the backyard next time. It had way more space than my room.

After Alexa left, I grabbed an apple from the kitchen and went to Dadi's room. She was sitting on her bed holding a big needle. Balls of colorful yarn were spread out around her.

"What are you doing?" I asked.

Dadi looked up with a frown. "Don't you say salaam in this house?"

"Salaam alaikum," I said, climbing onto the bed with her. "What are you doing?"

She held up the needle. It was thick and hooked at one end. "Crochet," she said.

"Is that English?" I asked. I knew a lot of big English words. But *crochet* sounded weird. Like maybe it was another language.

"French," Dadi replied.

I scowled. First Alexa talked about going to Paris and seeing the Eiffel Tower, and now Dadi was making something French with green yarn. Then I got distracted. "Green is my favorite color," I told her.

"Yes, I know."

"Sometimes I like red too, but most of the time I like green," I explained. "Light green, though, like leaves. Oh, but some leaves are dark green, and I don't like those at all . . ."

Dadi sighed and put the needle down. "Why aren't you in school, Marya?"

My mouth dropped open. "It's spring break! I told you before!"

"Oh, yes." Dadi patted my head. "A whole week to relax and have fun."

"Only there's no fun, because there's no Hanna," I grumbled.

"But there's that other girl. The one with golden hair."

"Alexa."

"Yes, that one. She's nice."

I didn't want to talk about Alexa. "What did you do for spring break when you were a kid, Dadi?" I asked.

Dadi smiled. "We didn't have spring break," she said. "But summer vacation was so much fun!"

I couldn't imagine Dadi having fun. She was always sitting in her room, watching Urdu dramas or reading books. "Really?" I asked suspiciously. "I'm going to need examples."

"Well, I climbed a lot of trees," she said. "And ran around the neighborhood with my friends."

My eyes got very big. "You did all that?"

"Yes." Dadi laughed. "I was young like you once."

I couldn't imagine Dadi as a young girl. How could she be my grandmother if she was eight years old like me?

"I wasn't your grandmother then." Dadi chuckled like she knew what I was thinking.

"I know." Then I had another thought. "Climbing? Running? Was there an adventure park in your neighborhood?"

Dadi looked at me. "What's this adventure park, eh?"

I flopped down onto the bed with a sigh. "Only the most awesome thing in the world."

Mama decided to clean the garage in the afternoon, and guess what? She made me help.

How can it be helping if I'm being forced to do it, that's what I'd like to know.

Okay, Sal was also there, but he was just leaning against the wall, playing on his Nintendo. I kicked his foot with mine. "Why are we even here?" I groaned.

"It's spring-cleaning, Marya," Mama said.

That made no sense because (a) What's spring got to do with cleaning? And (b) It's not my mess— why should I have to clean it up? I didn't even go into the garage. That's where Baba's car was kept at night. Plus, there was a whole section with piles of boxes and old furniture.

Mama stood near the boxes, hands on her hips. "We need to get rid of all this junk."

Ugh. This wasn't how I imagined spending my break.

My life was totally unfair.

Mama made me and Sal open each box and sort through the things inside. She got two giant trash bags. The one on the right was for garbage. The one on the left was for donations. "All old clothes and toys go in the donations pile," she told us. "Unless they're broken or torn."

"Hey," Sal said, picking up a blue dress. "This is your baby stuff, Marya!"

I scowled. The dress was tiny, with weird-looking ducks all over it. "No, it's not."

"Yup." Sal laughed. "Little Miss Ducky!"

I dropped a box of papers on the ground with a bang. "Shut up!"

"Marya!" Mama scolded me.

This was another very unfair part of my life. Mama always got mad at me, no matter what. She never cared that Sal was teasing me. All she cared about was that I didn't say bad words or yell too loud. "Sal called me Miss Ducky!" I cried.

"It's a compliment," Sal said. "Ducks are cool."

"So you be a duck then," I hissed. "Sal the Duck."

Mama glared at me. "Marya Khan! Stop joking around and get to work."

I wanted to scream, but I think that would put me in time-out or something. So I zipped up my lips and turned my back on Sal. "Where's Aliyah?" I mumbled. At least she didn't call me animal names. Mostly.

"She's at her friend Riley's house," Mama said. She took the blue dress from Sal and put it in the donation bag.

Now that we weren't talking to each other, we worked faster. We threw away a bunch of stuff, then mopped the floor and organized the shelves. The huge bag of donations made me feel better about this whole spring-cleaning business.

At least it meant some kids would get nice toys and clothes.

Mama gave me and Sal orange juice and potato chips as a reward for helping out. "I'm sorry I called you Miss Ducky," Sal whispered as we ate.

I grinned at him. "It's okay. I like ducks."

Aliyah came back from her friend's house. "We had so much fun!" she said. "Riley's got new skates, and she let me use her old ones. We skated up and down her street all afternoon!"

Just like that, my happy mood disappeared.

I wanted to stomp my foot—only too bad I was sitting down. Roller-skating was epic. Why was I stuck in the garage instead of playing with Hanna? This was the worst spring break ever.

"I hope you were both wearing helmets," Mama said.

"Yes, of course," Aliyah replied sweetly. "They

were the cool helmets, with mics so we could talk to each other."

I tried not to feel jealous, but it was no use. My chest was on fire with jealousy. "Alexa and I had fun too," I said loudly. "I ran around my room in twenty seconds!"

Mama smiled at me. "Twenty seconds, huh? That must be some world record."

I felt better as I imagined the headlines. *Marya Khan, Third Grader at Harold Smithers Elementary, Beats the World Record in Racing! The Whole Town Comes Out to Celebrate!*

MARYA KHAN
THIRD GRADER AT HAROLD SMITHERS
BEATS THE WORLD RECORD
IN RACING

#1

"I'm glad you and Alexa are getting along," Mama said to me. "You'll be spending lots of time with her this week."

My grin disappeared from my face. "What do you mean?"

"You'll see," Mama said mysteriously.

4

WORD OF THE DAY

MIRACLE

A wonderful event

 spent all night wondering about Mama's words. Spending lots of time with Alexa this week? What could be worse?

Then I started imagining all sorts of bad things happening, like my toys and books disappearing into thin air, or being chased by ducks in blue dresses, or pizza not even being invented.

Okay, so there were lots of worse things than spending time with my next-door neighbor. She wasn't too bad.

I felt better, mostly.

I woke up the next morning super tired, but at least school was off, so I could stay in bed. Only Mama had other ideas.

"Marya!" she yelled from downstairs. "Please come here, right now!"

I groaned. She'd better not be asking me to clean the garage some more.

I quickly brushed my teeth and changed my clothes, then went downstairs. Aliyah smirked from the hallway. "What did you do now?"

"Nothing!" I mumbled. "I think."

When I got to the living room, Mama was smiling. And next to her was . . . a miracle!

Also known as Hanna Gamal, my best friend. I shrieked and launched myself at her. "I can't believe it! You're here! You're here!"

Hanna hugged me back. "It's only been a few days since we saw each other," she said dryly.

"It felt like forever," I told her very serious-like. Aliyah watched us from the doorway, rolling her eyes as usual.

"How is your sister now, Hanna?" Mama asked.

"She's better, thank you," Hanna replied. "Her fever is gone, but the cough is still there."

"I'm sure your mother is very proud of you for being a good big sister," Mama told her. "Taking care of your siblings is so important."

I tried to think of Aliyah being a good big sister. She's never really taken care of me. But then I remembered the time she threw me a henna party, all because she felt bad for me. It was the best party of my entire life.

I went to Aliyah and hugged her too.

"Ew," she hissed. "What's the matter with you?"

"Just feeling happy," I said, then went back to Hanna. "Wanna play something?"

Mama held up her hand. "Not yet," she said. "There's another surprise coming."

"Like what?" One miracle was good enough for me. I didn't need any more.

Only too bad for me, because just then the doorbell rang and I heard Alexa call out, "Hello, Marya Khan!"

Mrs. Rhodes was drinking tea with Mama in the kitchen again. This was totally not the miracle I'd been looking for. It was strange because I didn't even know the two moms were friends. They were smiling and whispering like something amazing was going to happen.

Hanna, Alexa, and me stood in front of them with our arms crossed like a super-sassy girl army. "What's going on?" I asked loudly.

Mama smiled at me. "Lauren has a surprise for all three of you."

Wait, who was Lauren?

Mama pointed to Mrs. Rhodes, and I realized she was Lauren. Okay, that made sense. "Well?" Alexa asked, flipping her hair.

Mrs. Rhodes smiled even bigger than Mama. "We're all going to Skye Adventure Park this weekend!"

Whoa.

I was so not expecting that.

My mouth dropped open. Alexa squealed. "Oh my God, seriously? That's awesome!" She turned to me. "Right, Marya, isn't it awesome?"

I wanted to yell and squeal too, I really did. But

I just didn't understand it yet. Who exactly was going? Why?

Mrs. Rhodes took pity on me. "My job needs me to go out there for some interviews," she said. "So Faiza and I decided to make it a family vacation, because of spring break."

Faiza was my mama. Faiza Khan.

"But what about Hanna?" I whispered. I'd do anything to go to Skye, but not having Hanna there with me would make me very sad.

"I already spoke with Shirin," Mama said. "She agreed to let Hanna go with us as a thank-you for taking care of her sister."

I'm guessing Shirin was Hanna's mom. I never called her anything except Aunty. Weird how everyone's first names were coming out today.

"Really?" Hanna gasped.

"Really," Mrs. Rhodes and Mama said together.

"A family vacation?" I asked. "Like, everyone? Even Dadi?"

Mama nodded. "Even Dadi."

I imagined Dadi lying on a floatie in the middle

of the pool, drinking juice and wearing big sun-glasses. Oh, and her crochet would be right next to her. I'd get to show her all the most fun rides and the huge obstacle course. She'd like it a lot because she liked climbing trees and running in the street when she was little.

Knowing that Dadi was going with us made me believe the news more. Mama wouldn't joke about Dadi. "Yay!" I shouted, jumping up and down. "We're going to Skye Adventure Park!"

Alexa and Hanna shouted "yay!" and jumped up and down too.

"I don't know what the big deal is," Aliyah said from the doorway.

I stopped jumping and gave her a pitying look. She hadn't gone to Skye before with our cousins. I think she had the flu germs or something. "That's because you don't know how awesome Skye is."

Alexa and Hanna nodded. There was nothing better than Skye. Everybody knew that.

5

WORD OF THE DAY

SCHEME

To form a plan

oon after, Mrs. Rhodes went back to work.

Mama also went out. She owned a flower shop downtown, and she always went to garden stores on Tuesday mornings to get plants and things for the week.

Sometimes she got fertilizer, which was really stinky because it was made of poop. Gross but also kind of cool, right?

Just don't sit right next to it or you'll stink all day long. Trust me, I had experience with these things.

Alexa and Hanna sat in the living room, looking super excited. "I can't believe we're going to Skye," Hanna said, bouncing on the couch.

"It's really big," Alexa said. "We have to make sure we don't miss anything."

"I only want to do the obstacle course," I declared. "I don't care about the rest." Last time, I'd been too little for the obstacle course. It was my biggest disappointment.

There was no way I'd miss it this time.

"What about the water park?" Alexa asked, pouting.

Okay, yes. The water park would be amazing too. "Ugh, it's hard to decide!" Suddenly, I had a great idea. "We should have a plan."

"A plan for what?" Hanna asked, frowning.

I turned to Aliyah, who was working on her laptop. "Can I borrow that for a minute?" I asked as politely as possible.

Really, I was an angel.

Aliyah groaned like I'd asked for diamonds or pearls. "Okay, fine!" she finally hissed. "Just for a minute."

"Thanks." I beamed extra big, just to annoy her. Then I took the laptop and went to Skye's website.

We all leaned in to look at the screen. "Whoa, it's huge!" Aliyah said.

"Yup," I replied. "That's why we need a plan."

And guess what? I was the mistress of plans. I knew all about scheming and plotting. I was basically a plan queen.

The website showed all the things you could do at Skye. There was a water park (of course). There were also rides like the Ferris wheel (boring) and Tilt-A-Whirl (no thanks). The best thing of all? The obstacle course.

"There!" I jabbed my finger on the screen. "That's going to be the coolest."

Alexa leaned forward and sighed. "This is awesome."

It really was. The course was like something

out of a TV show. I shivered as I stared at it. There were ninja steps, rope swings, a mudslide, AND SO MUCH MORE!

Then I saw something even better. Something that made my heart pound. "It has a timer!" I practically shouted. "And there's a leaderboard with the fastest people's names!"

"Ooh," Alexa said.

"I want to be the fastest!" I said, smacking my fist on the coffee table. "I want my name on the top of the leaderboard."

"Why am I not surprised, Marya Khan?" Alexa asked dryly.

"We shouldn't compete against each other," Hanna protested. "We won't have fun."

I blinked. "What are you talking about? Racing is totally fun!"

Hanna shrugged. "So is playing together."

I turned to Alexa again. "What do you think?"

Alexa smiled big. I'd never asked her what she thought before. "We can race each other," she agreed. "But only if you go in the water park with me."

I looked at her with respect. This girl knew how to plan and scheme too. "It's a deal," I said.

We both looked at Hanna. She groaned. "Okay, fine!"

"Yay!" I grabbed paper from under the coffee table, and one of Aliyah's pencils. On the top of the paper, I wrote MARYA'S OBSTACLE COURSE in my very best handwriting.

"Why does it have to be *your* obstacle course?" Alexa asked.

I shrugged. "Because it's my plan."

Under the heading, I drew the course from the website.

"So beautiful," I crooned, smoothing my hand over the paper.

Aliyah laughed at me. "Really, Marya?"

I didn't bother to answer. Who cared if she thought I was weird?

I went back to my paper. Under the obstacle course, I drew three stick figures. I labeled them Alexa R., Marya K., and Hanna G. We all had smiley faces and muscles on our arms. I was in the front, with the hugest smile.

Oh, and I put a crown on my head too, just because.

When I was finished, I showed it to everyone. "We look good," Alexa said, pointing to the stick figures.

"We look like winners," Hanna added.

I gave her a look. "There can only be one winner," I said, pointing to my crown. "And her name is Marya Khan."

Alexa sniffed. "You wish. I'm the best athlete, remember?"

My shoulders slumped. I'd forgotten all about her home gym. "Oh yeah."

"Don't worry, Marya," Alexa said. "You can

practice a lot. Then you'll be almost as good as me."

I glared at her. Where would I practice? I didn't have a gym. I only had my tiny room and the backyard where Dadi grew her plants.

Then I got another brilliant idea.

"Your backyard is huge," I said to Alexa. "We can practice there."

Alexa frowned. "Like, how?"

I waved my paper in her face. "We can run and jump over things, maybe swing around from a rope . . ."

"As if Mama and Baba are going to let you swing from ropes in the backyard," Aliyah scoffed.

"We'll see." My heart jumped around in my chest. I knew exactly what I was going to do now. This was my best plan yet.

Operation Super Athlete.

I'd be the best athlete, better than Alexa with her home gym. Better than all the other kids who went to Skye.

I'd be the ultimate winner. I, Marya Khan, would run through the Skye obstacle course with the shortest time ever. Then my name would go at the very top of the leaderboard. Maybe they'd even give me prizes and throw me a parade and call me Marya the Super Athlete.

It would be awesome.

6

WORD OF THE DAY

RESEARCH

Study to find out

something

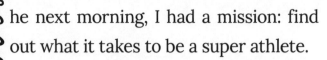he next morning, I had a mission: find out what it takes to be a super athlete.

I mean, let's face it. I didn't have a gym, but I'm sure I could do other things. There were probably lots of people who didn't have big mansions and gyms and rich parents, right?

I went to Baba's office after breakfast. He was working from home today. "Can I use your computer, please?" I asked very nicely. I even smiled to show him what a good girl I was.

Baba looked up. "Sure, my love. What do you need?"

"I want to look up something."

"Ah, you mean research." He pushed his laptop toward me. I stood on my tippy-toes and carefully typed out *how to be an athlete*. Miss Piccolo told us to have correct spelling and grammar when typing things. That way you got the correct information back.

I was great at spelling and grammar.

"An athlete, huh?" Baba said. "Is this for the adventure park?"

I nodded. "I want to be the fastest on the obstacle course."

Baba frowned. "You're going there to have fun," he said. "Don't make it into a competition."

"Can't I do both?" I asked.

I already knew the answer, though. Yes, I could definitely have fun *and* be the fastest. It was no big deal. I grinned to show Baba how excited I was.

He shook his head and smiled a little. "Typical Marya," he mumbled.

The computer gave me all sorts of results. My grin disappeared because this was way too much information. How was I supposed to find something in here? It was like all the boxes of junk in the garage. It would take hours to find something good.

"Check this out," Baba said, pointing to a link.

It was a health website for kids. Perfect! I clicked on the link and started reading.

How to be an athlete:

1. *Find your passion.*

That was easy. I already knew my passion was being the best at everything. Plus, Skye Adventure Park was also my passion. And obstacle courses. So basically, I was done with step number one already.

2. *Practice regularly.*

I could do that. I decided to tell Alexa that her backyard was definitely our new training place. She'd be okay with that. Probably.

3. *Eat and sleep well.*

Hey, I loved doing both of those things. Especially eating.

4. *It's okay to lose sometimes.*

Hmm. I didn't like this one. Plus, it was never going to happen. So I decided to ignore it.

I pushed away the computer. "Thank you, Baba!" I shouted, and skipped out the door. Operation Super Athlete was a go.

Next stop: the kitchen. Mama was still at home because her shop didn't open until eleven o'clock. "I need to eat a lot," I announced.

She leaned against the counter and looked at me. "Are you saying I don't feed you enough?"

"No." I rolled my eyes. "I'm saying I need to eat a lot because I'm an athlete now."

"Are you?" She rubbed her chin. "Well, what sorts of foods would you like, Miss Athlete?"

This was a good question. What were my favorite foods? "Pizza, obviously," I began.

"Obviously."

"Oh, and cookies." My stomach rumbled. "And pancakes. Cakes in general would be good."

Mama sighed. "Look, Marya. If you want to grow strong and healthy, you can't stuff yourself with those kinds of foods. They're unhealthy."

I blinked. Seriously? Pizza and cookies were unhealthy? Why hadn't I known this before?

"You need to eat lots of fruits and vegetables to be healthy," Mama continued.

My heart sank. Fruits were okay, but veggies? No thanks. "What else?" I asked.

"Protein too, if you're going to be exercising a lot."

"What's that?" I wrinkled my nose. Protein sounded like a very disgusting vegetable.

"Don't worry, it's chicken or turkey," Mama said, laughing. "And also daal."

Phew. Daal was my favorite. "Okay!" I said. "Make daal for lunch."

Mama crossed her arms and raised an eyebrow. I wish I knew how she did that. Whenever I tried, both of my eyebrows rose at once. "Really?" Mama asked.

"Please?" I begged.

"Much better." Mama turned away. "Daal for lunch sounds like a great idea."

I grinned. It wasn't every day someone thought my ideas were great.

Third stop: a place to train. I went into the living room to call Alexa and Hanna. It was time to come up with a training plan.

And I didn't mean a gym. I meant an actual obstacle course.

Operation Super Athlete was going to be Super Awesome.

7

WORD OF THE DAY

PRACTICING

Doing something

over and over

"re you sure about this, Marya?" Alexa asked.

"Of course." I rolled my eyes. "I thought you were brave."

"I am very brave," she replied, tossing her head like a horse. "One time I got stung by a bee and didn't even cry."

I looked at her with my mouth open. Beestings were the worst.

"Not even a little bit?" Hanna asked.

"Nope."

It was Thursday morning, right after my very healthy breakfast of wheat pancakes (yum), yogurt (eh), and cranberry juice (yuck). I even finished the juice to prove how much I wanted to be an athlete.

Now we were standing in Alexa's backyard, and let me tell you, this place was huge. There was a patio with fancy furniture and a swimming pool. I'd never seen any other house with a pool before. There was a little fence around it, but you could still see the water, all blue and shimmery.

"The tile in our swimming pool is from Greece," Alexa told us with a smirk.

I rolled my eyes again. Who cared where the tile came from?

"Ooh," Hanna said. "I like Greek salad."

"Me too!" Alexa replied, and they high-fived each other.

"Forget Greece," I grumbled. "Let's get started with training!"

"Better be careful, girls!" Dadi called out from the patio.

Dadi was our babysitter today. She sat on a patio chair, working on her crochet with that dreadful hooked needle and balls of green yarn.

Don't ask me what she was making. I had no clue.

Hanna waved to her. "We will!"

We went over to the other side of the pool.

"Ta-da!" Alexa cried, jumping up and down.

My eyes opened big like the full moon. There were all kinds of obstacles in the grass. Small step stools to jump over. A balance beam made of wood. And guess what? There were actual ninja steps too!

"Wow," I whispered, very impressed.

"Did you do all this by yourself?" Hanna asked, her eyes wide.

Alexa shrugged. "My gardener helped me."

But that wasn't everything. Alexa proudly pointed to a big tree. "Check this out," she said.

The tree had a thick rope coming down from a branch. "Cool rope," I said. Climbing ropes were definitely on my Operation Super Athlete list.

"Not that," Alexa said. She pointed again.

I looked closer. On the fence behind the tree were a bunch of wooden things stuck out in different sections. They looked like . . .

"Is that a rock wall?" Hanna gasped.

"Kind of," Alexa replied.

My eyes got even bigger. It definitely looked

like a rock wall, only much smaller. But it didn't matter, because it would still help me practice.

"Perfect!" Hanna cried.

"I can use this to climb over to your house whenever I want, Marya!" Alexa said, grinning.

"Er, please don't."

"Why?" Alexa kept grinning. "We're friends, right? We can have sleepovers and everything."

I stared at her in horror. Was she serious? Did I have to lock my window in case she came in without permission? She looked a bit strange with that huge grin. Plus, she wasn't wearing a fancy dress for once. She had on jeans and a plain white T-shirt.

Maybe she was an alien disguised as Alexa R. Maybe she had green skin and creepy-crawly bug eyes, only she was hiding it with some magical alien technology.

That would actually be pretty awesome. Alexa the Alien.

Hanna started laughing. "You're funny, Alexa."

Alexa did a bow. "Thank you!"

Okay, so no alien Alexa. Only regular, slightly-annoying-but-also-kind-of-okay Alexa.

I looked at the obstacles in the backyard. Joking around was not how Operation Super Athlete was supposed to work. I needed to give Hanna and Alexa a push.

I headed to a long patch of empty grass. "Race you to the rock wall!"

We spent the rest of the afternoon practicing.

Well, Hanna and Alexa just ran around and had fun. They laughed and pushed each other, and then laughed some more.

I focused on Operation Super Athlete. There was no laughing in that. It was super-serious business because it was all about winning.

W-I-N-N-I-N-G

That wasn't a big word, but it should have been in my Word of the Day diary anyway, on account of how important it was. Winning gave you the bestest feeling in the whole world, almost as good as tight hugs from Mama and Baba.

You know what *was* in my Word of the Day diary? *Succeeding.* It meant coming in first and winning prizes. Maybe even a crown.

So far, I'd won the first section of the obstacle course, which was running. I guess that was expected. I was a great runner. Alexa had won in the ninja steps, and Hanna had come first in the balance beam.

That wasn't so expected. Hanna hardly ever played sports except for soccer. That's because her dad used to be a soccer player in Egypt.

"You're really good at the balance beam," I told her, trying not to feel jealous.

She shrugged like it was no big deal. "My feet are quick."

"But you won," I reminded her. How could she forget?

Hanna shrugged again. "I guess."

"You were close too, Marya," Alexa said, patting my head like I was a baby.

Close? I'd actually come in last. I fell off the balance beam three times. Ugh. It was horrible.

"Yeah, we all won," Hanna added cheerfully. "Yay us!"

I stomped my feet as I walked away to the ninja steps. Why was Hanna cheering? I didn't want anyone to cheer for me if I came in last. I only wanted cheers and clapping and *hooray, Marya!* when I came in first.

Was that too much to ask?

8

WORD OF THE DAY

EXHAUSTED

Very, very tired

round four o'clock, Dadi put down her crochet needles. "I've run out of green yarn," she complained.

I'd run out of energy, but I wasn't going to tell anyone. It was against the rules of Operation Super Athlete to complain.

Alexa and Marya had stopped practicing half an hour ago.

"Come on, Marya," Hanna called out. "Have some rest."

She was lying on the grass, and Alexa sat near her legs. They looked tired. I was dangling from the tree rope, so it wasn't my best look. Still, I shook my head. "Can't," I panted. "Have to . . . practice."

"You sound like a zombie," Alexa said, giggling.

I scowled. I didn't sound anything like a zombie, thank you very much. "A super athlete, you mean."

"Why are you so intent on winning?" Alexa asked. Then she paused. "That means 'determined.'"

I scowled some more. It was hard to do when you were dangling from a tree, but I managed it. "I know what *intent* means."

Secretly, I wondered if Alexa also had a Word of the Day diary. That would make her even more like me, which was a strange thought. So, I didn't think about it.

"Yes, why, Marya?" Hanna asked.

I dropped from the rope and sat down on the grass. My hands hurt something bad. "Because I want to be the best."

"Being the best is overrated," Alexa said sadly. "Look at my dad. He's the best salesman in the city. He got an award for it and everything. But he's never home, so it's not a good thing at all."

I sighed. It was hard to stay mad at Alexa when she talked about her family.

"I'll be the best, but I'll still spend time with you two," I told her, rolling my eyes.

She smiled. "That's good, Marya Khan. I like spending time with you."

I blinked very fast. I had no idea what to say.

Thankfully, Baba saved the day. He stepped into the backyard, smiling widely. "Hello, girls, you look exhausted!"

"Finally!" Dadi grumbled. "What took you so long?"

"I was working," Baba explained. "But I stopped to take you girls for ice cream. Seems like you had a hard day of practice."

I jumped up. How did he know I needed some ice cream to make me forget my aching muscles?

"Yay!" Hanna squealed. "I'm so hot."

"Thank you, Mr. Khan," Alexa said very politely.

Dadi stood up slowly. "Not me. I want to go home and drink some tea."

I helped her with her yarn and needles. I didn't want her falling down in Alexa's backyard because she had too many things to carry. "Thank you, Marya jaan," she said, smiling. "Isn't it pretty?" She held up the thing she was making. It was bright green and strange-looking, like a cross between a sock and a sweater.

"Er, sure," I mumbled.

We helped Dadi take her stuff next door while Baba waited in his car. The three of us trooped into my house. Mama took one look at us and said "Wash up, please!" very sternly.

There was a small bathroom near the front

door. Alexa, Hanna, and I took turns washing our hands and faces. "Use soap!" Mama called from outside.

"Your mom is strict," Alexa whispered, giggling. She looked like a regular girl with her jeans and T-shirt, all muddy from playing in the yard.

Practicing. Not playing.

"She's nice," Hanna whispered back.

I smiled because it was very true. Mama was the best. If there was an award for Super Mom, she'd definitely win. She took care of our whole family, plus ran her flower shop with that rusty old van and poop fertilizer. It was enough to drive anyone nuts.

And now she was making me super-athlete food too.

When I left the bathroom, I went straight to Mama and hugged her.

"What do you want, Marya?" she asked suspiciously.

"Nothing," I said. "You just got an award for Super Mom."

"Moms don't need awards," she replied. "We just need obedient kids."

"What does that mean, Mrs. Khan?" Hanna asked.

"*Obedient*? It means to do what you're told."

Hanna and Alexa both laughed. "Marya's not obedient," Alexa said.

I crossed my arms. "I am!" I growled.

Mama smiled. "You try your best, Marya. That's all I want." She opened the fridge. "How about some healthy snacks for you athletes? I have carrots and celery sticks with ranch. Oh, and also raisins. What do you think?"

I shivered in disgust. Raisins reminded me of little ants. "No thanks. Baba's taking us for ice cream."

She turned back to me and raised that magical eyebrow again. "Really? I'm quite sure ice cream isn't athlete food."

I didn't want to hear this right now. I would literally faint if I didn't have ice cream. It was essential to my survival.

Essential means super-duper important.

"I like raisins," Alexa said.

Nope, not happening. I pulled Alexa and Hanna out of the kitchen. "Let's go!" I yelled. "Before Mama makes me eat healthy food."

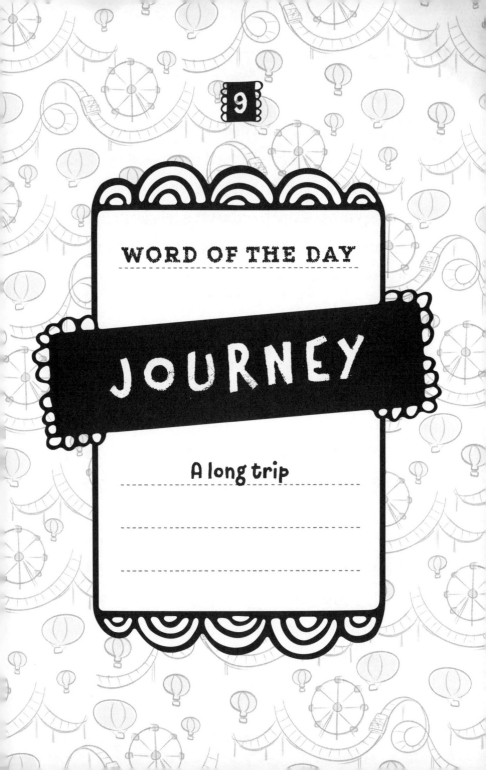

9

WORD OF THE DAY

JOURNEY

A long trip

It took forever for Saturday to arrive.

We were going to Skye Adventure Park today, in case anyone had forgotten. Only I couldn't ever forget. I'd practiced in Alexa's backyard again yesterday, even when my legs hurt and the palms of my hands were all scratched up.

Hanna and Alexa had watched me from the deck the whole time. They even clapped and cheered for me.

Operation Super Athlete was a success so far.

I felt ready to win Skye's obstacle course and get my name on the leaderboard. Then my life would be complete.

The Skye people better be ready to throw me a parade. Or maybe a big party. I'd be okay with either.

Breakfast was paratha and eggs for everyone else, but a bowl of fruit and yogurt for me. "How unfair!" I grumbled.

"Paratha is made up of carbs and oil, Marya," Aliyah said with a smirk. "It's not athlete food."

Oh yeah. I'd told my family about healthy eating

for athletes. Aliyah and Sal had laughed at me so hard. "You'll never be able to eat healthy," Sal had said. "You like cookies too much."

"Oatmeal cookies are healthy," Mama protested.

It was nice of her to take my side against my evil siblings. So I nodded and said nothing, even though I didn't like oatmeal cookies at all.

If it meant being a super athlete, I could eat oatmeal cookies.

Maybe.

Probably.

"We're leaving in thirty minutes," Baba reminded us at the breakfast table.

I gobbled up my breakfast and looked through my backpack.

I'd already packed, but I checked again just to be sure. Extra clothes. My swimming leggings and shirt for the water park. A floppy hat. A bottle of sunscreen.

What was I missing?

Oh! I remembered something I'd seen a few days ago. I went to look in the garage. The bag of donations was still in the corner, waiting for Baba to take to the shelter. I quickly opened it and searched inside.

Found it! It was a pair of black gloves, only without the fingers. They were Aliyah's a long time ago, but now her hands were too big. But guess what? They fit me perfectly.

It was weird to be wearing gloves that didn't cover your fingertips. Who even thought that was a good idea? Only they were nice and soft, and they'd keep my hands from getting hurt when I hung from the monkey bars or ropes.

I was a genius, probably.

In thirty minutes, there was a honk outside. I rushed to the front door and flung it open. "They're here!" I screamed.

Mrs. Rhodes and Alexa sat in a sleek white car. It looked fancy, just like the Rhodes family. Alexa leaned out of the window and waved madly. "Hi, Marya!" she yelled. "Aren't you excited for our voyage?"

"What?" I wanted to stomp my foot that she knew a word I didn't.

"You know," she said. "Our journey. Our expedition."

"You mean road trip? Of course I'm ready!" I turned toward my house. "Everybody, come on! Let's go!"

My family came outside. Sal, Aliyah, Baba, Mama, and finally, Dadi. Everyone had their own bag, plus Baba was carrying a cooler of water and snacks.

I waited for him to go to his car, but instead he went to Mama's van, the one that belonged to her flower shop.

I gulped. I hated this van. It always smelled stinky because of all the gross things Mama carried in it, like fertilizer and mulch. One time she

even put rotting flowers in it, to throw them out in the big trash place outside of town.

"Can't we go in your car?" I begged.

He shook his head. "There's not enough room in my car for everyone."

My shoulders slumped. Stinky van it was.

Baba put the cooler in the back while Dadi got into the front. I dragged myself into the middle seat. Surprisingly, it wasn't stinky. Mama must have taken it to the car wash this week.

"Thank you, Mama," I whispered, even though she couldn't hear me.

"I'll come with you, Marya!" Alexa shouted. She got out of her mom's car and into the van, right next to me. She was carrying a fancy white backpack with a kitten on the front.

"What about Hanna?" I asked.

"We'll pick her up on the way," Baba replied.

So basically, I'd have annoying Alexa on one side and bestie Hanna on the other. They would balance each other out.

Sal and Aliyah climbed into the back behind us. "Hey, Mar," Sal said, flicking my ponytail.

"Stop!" I squealed.

"You stop being a baby," Aliyah said.

Baba got into the driver's seat. "You kids need to behave, please," he said in a stern voice. "I can't have fighting in the back while I'm driving."

Sal, Aliyah, and I glared at each other, but we stopped fighting. We always listened to Baba when he used that tone.

Mama got into the white car with Mrs. Rhodes. Baba started the van and we began driving.

Alexa grinned. "Road trip!" she whispered happily.

10

WORD OF THE DAY

MISERABLE

Very unhappy or sad

Skye Adventure Park was two hours away. Aliyah closed her eyes and went to sleep.

Baba put on some low music, and Dadi took out her crochet. "My scarf is almost done," she said happily.

"Who are you making it for?" Baba asked her.

Dadi shrugged. "I haven't decided yet," she replied.

I smiled secretly because my detective skills were at work again. I loved the color green. Dadi loved me. So basically, this scarf was for me.

I was, like, ninety-nine percent sure.

"What do you want to play, girls?" Sal said from the back. I turned around to look at him. He had an evil grin on his face, which meant he wanted to play a tough game.

Something he'd win and I'd lose.

"Play?" Alexa asked, frowning.

"Yeah, like a road trip game," Hanna said.

Alexa looked confused. All of a sudden, I

realized what her problem was. "You've never been on a road trip before?" I gasped.

She looked down at her lap. "No," she said softly. "Only plane trips. Oh, and one time we took a train ride that was so long, we had to sleep on the train in little bunk beds."

I huffed. Queen Alexa was always doing cool, fancy things like that. But then I noticed she didn't look happy about any of it. Not even sleeping on a bunk bed on a train.

Maybe she liked cars more. "Road trip games are fun," I said nicely.

"Can you teach me?" she asked shyly.

"I'll teach you," Sal said. "We can play the color game. That's easy."

Please! The color game was for babies. You chose a color and then found things on the road with that color. Like red stop signs and red cars and red flowers on the side of the road. It was boring. "Let's play Would You Rather," I suggested.

Hanna clapped. "Ooh, I like that one!"

"Okay, I'll go first," Sal said. "Would you rather eat an insect or eat poop?"

"Ew!" all three of us girls shouted.

"Not so loud, please!" Baba said from the front.

"Insect, obviously," I said. There was no way on earth I was ever eating poop. Even if I was starving.

"Me too," Sal said. "Chocolate-covered crickets, to be precise."

Hanna looked like she was going to puke.

I seriously doubted Sal would eat something so yucky. Still, I didn't want Hanna getting sick, so I nudged her. "You next."

"Hmm," she said. "Would you rather have the power to be invisible or super strong?"

"Invisible," Alexa said quickly.

"Me too," Sal said, and they gave each other high fives.

Seriously? That made no sense. "I'd rather be super strong," I told them. "I'd be the best athlete and they'd give parades in my honor and I'd wear a crown."

Alexa stared at me. "Crowns are for kings and queens. Not weight lifters."

Weight lifters? I had no idea what she was talking about. Super-strong people ruled the world. Why was she always trying to confuse me?

I decided to give Alexa an easy question, on account of this being her first road trip. "Hey, Alexa, would you rather live in a huge mansion or a small apartment?"

I knew exactly what she was going to say. She had a gym and a swimming pool and she wore pretty dresses most of the time and she traveled on fancy trains. She loved being rich. She'd totally choose the mansion.

Only she shocked me. Her eyes filled with tears and she turned to look out the window. Basically, she looked miserable. "Big mansions can be very lonely, Marya Khan."

Okay then.

There was a weird silence in the car. Baba frowned at me in the rearview mirror. Sal pulled my ponytail really hard. "Look what you did!" he whispered. "Bad Marya."

My head hurt. I gulped and slinked down in my seat. I actually had no idea what I'd done. But there was no way I was going to apologize.

Dadi turned around. "Don't be sad, little girl. Here, take this."

I sat up straight. What was Dadi giving her?

It was green and woolly and long.

It was a green crochet scarf. The one I thought Dadi was making for me.

Alexa sniffed and took the scarf. "Thank you," she whispered. Then she turned to me. "It's okay, Marya. I'm not mad at you."

I looked away from her, because guess what? I was a little mad at *her* now.

Soon, Baba took an exit. A sign said SKYE ADVENTURE PARK: FIVE MILES.

I grabbed Hanna's arm. "Look!"

Sal leaned forward. "They spelled *sky* wrong."

"It's named after the founder's daughter, genius," I replied. "Her name is Skye with an *E*."

"Lucky girl," Hanna said. "She has a whole entire park named after her."

I imagined a theme park called Marya's Adventure Park. Only Sal wouldn't be allowed inside.

Ha! He'd beg and plead, but I'd stand at the entrance, saying, "Nope, sorry. Go build your own park somewhere else." Except Mama would probably punish me and Baba would shake his head at me in that disappointed way he had.

Maybe I'd let Sal in, but only if he paid me a million dollars.

Hanna would get in free though. And Alexa too, since I'd made her cry.

I didn't know how long five miles was, but it

felt like a million years. I felt like my whole body was going to launch out of the car and whoosh down the road.

Only too bad because Baba was driving slower now, on account of being on a regular road instead of a highway. And there were a hundred stoplights. Then Aliyah woke up with a yawn. "Are we there yet?"

"Almost," Baba replied.

Aliyah yawned again, kind of like a lion or a bear. Something with claws and sharp teeth. "I need to go to the bathroom," she announced. "Baba, can you stop?"

"NO!" I yelled.

"Excuse me?" Aliyah gasped like the world was ending.

"We're almost there," I said in a less yelling voice. "You can wait."

Her eyes narrowed. "I wasn't talking to you," she hissed. "Baba, can you stop somewhere, please?"

Baba kept driving. "Just ten more minutes, Aliyah. You can go to the bathroom at Skye."

I sighed in relief. For once, someone was on my side.

Only then Aliyah pulled my hair and told me I was a meanie, so I guess my life was totally unfair once again.

I couldn't wait to get out of this car and away from everyone.

11

WORD OF THE DAY

CHAMPION

The winner of a

big competition

kye Adventure Park was huge. I could see the tops of the roller coasters and the Ferris wheel. A billboard had a picture of a little girl in pigtails and overalls. There was a bubble coming out from her mouth like a cartoon, saying WELCOME TO SKYE.

I thought this day would never come. My heart was thumping extra loud in my chest, like it was telling me *Go in, Marya, go in.*

I told my heart to wait, because Mrs. Rhodes had to talk to the ticket people. Her job had sent her to interview some people at the park, or something. I didn't really care. She could wear a clown suit and dance around if she liked. All I wanted was to go inside and get my adventure started.

"Are you excited, Marya?" Alexa whispered, squeezing my arm.

I ignored her, mainly because around her neck she was wearing the green scarf Dadi had given her. It was way too big, and it reached all the way up to her chin. She looked silly. "You should put that away," I told her angrily. "It will get caught in one of the rides."

"Good idea," Alexa said. She took off the scarf and put it very gently inside her kitten backpack. She was wearing jeans today, just like Hanna and I. "Now we match."

I rolled my eyes. "What's in that bag anyway?"

"Clothes and snacks." She snapped her fingers. "Ooh, and a first aid kit."

I shook my head at how silly she was. "This isn't a dangerous place, Alexa. You can't get hurt here."

"You never know, Marya. It's good to be prepared."

Just then, Mrs. Rhodes waved at us. "We can go in now!"

"Hooray!" Sal shouted, and raced to the entrance.

I forgot all about Alexa and raced after Sal. There was no way he was getting inside first.

"Be careful, Marya!" Mama called out.

I guess she didn't know that super athletes didn't need to be careful. We needed to be bold and brave. Like the Hulk.

Only not green. Green wasn't my favorite color anymore.

The man at the entrance gave us wristbands to wear and maps of the park. We went inside, and I tried very hard not to cry with happiness. It was a magical place. There weren't too many people

except for us, on account of it being early in the morning. I'm sure it would get crowded later on.

"Whoa," Aliyah whispered.

I was speechless, so I didn't even say that. I just nodded.

Baba split us into two groups. He was going to take us kids for fun things like the obstacle course and scary rides—yay!

Mama and Dadi were going to sit on lounge chairs nearby and watch us—boo!

"You should come with us on the rides, Mama," I said.

Mama nodded. "I need to call a customer about some roses they ordered," she said. "I'll join you later."

I hugged her goodbye. The next time she'd be seeing me, I'd be a champion.

I turned toward the obstacle course. It was time to put Operation Super Athlete to the test.

The obstacle course was just like I remembered. The ninja steps, the balance beam, the rock wall . . . even the waterfall in the distance. It was all spectacular.

I put down my backpack and pulled out my gloves. "Ready?"

Alexa put on a cloth headband, the kind that kept sweat away. She looked cool.

"Are you sure we should compete with each other?" Hanna asked softly. She wasn't wearing anything extra like Alexa and I. She looked like her regular self. "I just want to have fun."

"This is going to be so much fun," I promised her.

Sal's eyes became round. "Wait, you three are racing?"

I led the way to the timer. It had a big red button that said PRESS FOR TIMER. I frowned. "Where's the board with all the winners' names?"

Alexa tapped my shoulder. "I don't think it's working, Marya," she whispered.

I turned to where she was pointing. On a wall was the leaderboard, but instead of having names and minutes, it was completely blank.

"I guess it's broken or something," Sal said.

I blinked furiously. How did everyone know who was the best? The fastest? How did they celebrate the super athletes?

I wanted to stomp my foot and scream, but everyone was looking at me with sad eyes. Like they felt sorry for me.

"It's fine," Baba said. "You should still use the timer. I'll be the judge."

I perked up a little. "Will I get a prize if I win?"

"Sure," Baba said. "They have chocolate sundaes the size of boats here."

My eyes grew round as I imagined a sundae that big, shaped like a boat. Maybe it would have oars made of wafers. And a cherry on top of the sail.

Oh, and a chocolate statue of me, Marya Khan.

I ran to the start of the obstacle course. Alexa and Hanna followed me. Hanna also put her backpack down, but Alexa was still wearing hers.

I didn't care. It would make her slower. It would make her lose, probably.

To my surprise, Sal and Aliyah also joined. I

wanted to say they were too big and their legs were too long, and that was totally unfair. But then I remembered all my practice. All the wheat pancakes.

I'd win. I just knew it.

I looked at the course carefully. I remembered the steps I'd found on Aliyah's laptop:

Step 1: race line

Step 2: ninja steps

Step 3: rope swing

Step 4: rock wall

Step 5: balance beam

Step 6: mudslide

Step 7: stone jump

Step 8: waterfall

Easy peasy lemon squeezy.

"If you fall, you're out of the race," Aliyah told me.

I gulped. Okay, maybe not very easy peasy. Still, I gave her a thumbs-up. I wouldn't fall. I was Super Athlete Marya.

"Ready, set, go!" Baba yelled, hitting the timer.

I raced to the end of the zone. I pumped my legs and pushed my body forward, and guess what? I got to the end way before everyone else. "Yessss!" I whispered to myself.

Too bad there was no time to celebrate. Aliyah with her long legs was coming right behind me. I

quickly ran to the ninja steps. They were wobbly, but that was okay. The wooden pieces that Alexa's gardener had used were wobbly too. I jumped from one to the other really quickly.

Basically like a ninja.

Aliyah yelled behind me. I knew without looking that she'd fallen off the ninja steps. That meant she was out of the race.

Too bad for her, but hooray for me. One less person to compete against.

At the end of the steps, I took a deep breath.

One Mississippi. Two Mississippi. Three Mississippi.

"Hi, Marya!" Alexa was right behind me. And Hanna wasn't far behind her. Yikes. I grabbed the rope swing. There were two of them, and Alexa grabbed the other one. "Those gloves were a great idea," she said, panting.

"Thanks," I said, also panting.

Then I pushed myself off the rope and jumped into the sandbox at the bottom.

Only I landed all wrong, with my leg twisted under me.

Ouch.

12

WORD OF THE DAY

OUTSTANDING

Something that

stands out and

gets noticed

re you okay, Marya?" Hanna shouted from behind me on the rope swing. Sal was right behind her and Alexa.

I stood up quickly. My ankle was sore, but there was no time to lose. Baba was watching me with his hands on his hips. If I didn't act like I was okay, he'd make me leave the race.

Super athletes never quit. Even I knew that.

I hobbled super fast to the rock wall. This was my favorite part because I felt like a spider climbing up the waterspout. I grabbed the first rock and hauled myself up. My ankle twinged, but I totally ignored it.

From the corner of my eye, I saw Sal fall to the ground. Normally, I'd be happy, but right then I had bigger problems. Also known as the twinge in my ankle.

Rock number two. Another twinge.

Rock number three. Double, triple twinge. Lots of twinges that got worse and worse.

"You can do it, Marya!" Mama shouted.

I turned and waved to her and Dadi. I was so proud that they were looking at me.

Everyone was looking at me, even people who I didn't know. Guess what? There was quite a crowd in the park now.

No pressure, right?

Quickly, I stepped on the fourth rock, and AAAAHHHH, my ankle caught fire.

Well, not real fire. Just . . . very painful. Full of torture, basically.

I started breathing heavy. What if my whole leg fell off? What if I crumpled to the ground and they had to shut down Skye because of an injured girl?

Everybody at Skye would hate me. Even I would hate me.

I looked down. Alexa and Hanna were right under me now. I guess they'd caught up with me while I was trying not to die. They looked proud, which was weird. If someone was ahead of me in a race, I'd be totally jealous.

"You're doing great, Marya!" Alexa yelled.

Only I really wasn't because of the fire in my stupid ankle. I bit my lip, but secretly I felt like crying.

No crying, Marya. Super athletes don't cry.

"What's the matter?" Hanna asked, frowning.

"Why do you think something's the matter?" I mumbled.

"Because you're my best friend and I can tell."

"Oh. My ankle's really hurting . . ." Then I stopped talking, because why did I just mention this? They'd know I was weak and they'd take their chance to win.

"Don't worry, I'll help you get to the top," Hanna said cheerfully.

"Me too," Alexa said, even more cheerfully.

My eyes popped open. "You're not supposed to help me. We're competitors."

Alexa shrugged. "We can work together."

"Yeah, ever heard of a team?" Hanna said, smiling.

I stared at them. I really, really wanted to win even if there wasn't a prize or a crown. Except right now I was hanging from a rock wall, surrounded by my best friend and my best sometimes-enemy. Was that teamwork? Probably.

It was strange, but also fun. "Okay," I whispered. "We can be a team."

"Yay!" Hanna got so excited she bumped into my leg.

"Ow!" I hissed.

"You need some medicine," Alexa said. She reached into her backpack with one hand and pulled out a tube. "I told you it's best to be prepared."

Okay, so the kitten backpack was a good idea. Who knew?

Alexa rubbed some ointment on my ankle, and I sighed in relief. "Is that a magic potion?" I asked. "Are you a witch, Alexa?"

She giggled.

"Now let's get down from here," Hanna ordered.

The three of us slowly climbed back down the rock wall. I stayed in the middle of Hanna and Alexa. I kept thinking about the timer, and how slow we were being. Ugh, all my plans were wiped out.

Then I told myself to forget it. Maybe that athlete website was right. Sometimes it was okay to lose, I guess.

Right before we got to the balance beam, Alexa stopped and pulled something out of her backpack. Something long and green.

Dadi's crochet scarf. "Wrap this around your ankle," she told me.

I looked at her like she was off her rocker.

"Do it!"

I took the scarf and wrapped it around my ankle. "So soft," I muttered.

Maybe Dadi had put some magic spell in the yarn.

We walked together to the balance beam. Hanna took my hand and went ahead of me. "Be careful," she said.

Alexa was behind me, and she kept her hand on my back the whole time.

We went all the way across the balance beam, and guess what? I didn't wobble even once.

Maybe it was the magical scarf.

Probably it was my friends holding me so tight.

From the beam, we slid into the gross mudslide. We were still holding hands, even though my ankle felt better. "Ew!" Alexa screamed.

Hanna and I looked at each other and giggled. Miss Fancy Dress Alexa was all muddy and slimy!

"Look, Alexa," I said, holding up an arm dripping with gooey mud. "We match!"

She stuck her tongue out at me, and I giggled some more.

From the mudslide, we went across a little pond with stepping stones. We were so slippery that we really needed to hold on to each other now.

One-two-three-four. "This is so fun, Marya!" Alexa said, grinning.

I gave her a thumbs-up. Her face was all brown with mud, but her eyes shone bright blue.

We got to the end of the pond without falling, which was basically a miracle. Then we found ourselves at a small waterfall. "Um," I said.

Did they expect us to go under the water? How deep was it? Would there be sharks?

Hanna pushed me a little. "You go first."

I went into the water, thankful that it only came up to the top of my legs. I yelled because it was super cold like melted ice cream. Hanna came next and she yelled too. Alexa was third. We just stood in the water while all the mud washed off us.

And we didn't even shiver because everything was so fun that we forgot to be cold.

I gasped. "This is better than the water park."

"Way better," Hanna agreed.

Alexa pointed to a big green flag at the other side of the waterfall. "Guess we finished the obstacle course."

My face turned into a giant grin. I'd done it! Completed one entire obstacle course at Skye!

Baba was waiting for us at the edge of the pond with Sal and Aliyah. "So, who came in first?" Baba asked.

I shrugged. "I guess it was a tie," I said.

"What happened to Operation Super Athlete?"

I looked at my teammates. "It turned into Operation Super Athletes," I replied, making sure I sounded out the last S very loudly, like a snake.

Alexa and Hanna laughed.

Mama came running up to us. "Marya, is your ankle okay?"

I looked down. I'd forgotten all about my ankle.

Dadi's scarf was all wet and gross, but my ankle

felt fine. "The crochet saved me!" I told her.

"And us," Alexa protested, nudging me. "We saved you too."

"So was the obstacle course as good as you hoped?" Mama asked.

Was she kidding? "It was outstanding!" I practically shouted.

"Ooh, outstanding, eh?" Baba said, smiling. "Glad to hear, Miss Dictionary."

"I'm starving," I announced. "Can I have some non-healthy food please?"

"It's not time for lunch yet," Mama said. "I'll order the pizza. In the meantime, why don't you kids try out some of the rides?"

"Okay." I peeled off the scarf and gave it to her. I'm sure she'd figure out how to dry it for Alexa. She always knew everything.

Hanna dragged me to the Ferris wheel. "I want to ride that one."

I took Alexa's hand. "I have an idea," I said. "First one to finish all the rides gets a crown made of pizza boxes."

"You want to race again?" Alexa asked, shocked. "Didn't you learn your lesson, Marya Khan?"

I gave her an evil smile. "Once an athlete, always an athlete."